She'll Be Coming
Around the Mou

She'll be coming around the mountain
when she comes.
She'll be coming around the mountain
when she comes.

She'll be coming around the mountain.
She'll be coming around the mountain.
She'll be coming around the mountain
when she comes.

She will drive a new red race car
when she comes.
She will drive a new red race car
when she comes.

She will drive a new red race car.
She will drive a new red race car.
She will drive a new red race car
when she comes.

She'll be wearing cool sunglasses
when she comes.
She'll be wearing cool sunglasses
when she comes.

She'll be wearing cool sunglasses.
She'll be wearing cool sunglasses.

She'll be wearing cool sunglasses
when she comes.

We will all go out to meet her
when she comes.
We will all go out to meet her
when she comes.

We will all go out to meet her.
We will all go out to meet her.
We will all go out to meet her
when she comes.

We will play some happy music
when she comes.
We will play some happy music
when she comes.

We will play some happy music.
We will play some happy music.
We will play some happy music
when she comes.

We will all have cake and ice cream
when she comes.

We will all have
cake and ice cream
when she comes.

We will all have cake and ice cream.
We will all have cake and ice cream.
We will all have cake and ice cream
when she comes.

We will have a great big party
when she comes.
We will have a great big party
when she comes.

We will have a great big party.
We will have a great big party.
We will have a great big party
when she comes.

What fun!